Hot Fudge Hero

Hot Fudge Hero

by **Pat Brisson**
Illustrated by
Diana Cain Bluthenthal

SCHOLASTIC INC.
New York Toronto London Auckland Sydney

In loving memory of Sr. Mary Hugh, R. S. M.,
my second-grade teacher, who taught me to read.
Thank you, Sister. —P. B.

For my brothers, Mike and Mark,
who inspirit Bertie —Lovingly, D. C. B.

ISBN 0-590-03094-9

Text copyright © 1997 by Pat Brisson.
Illustrations copyright © 1997 by Diana Cain Bluthenthal.
All rights reserved. Published by Scholastic Inc.,
555 Broadway, New York, NY 10012, by arrangement with
Henry Holt and Company, Inc.

SCHOLASTIC and associated logos are trademarks and/or
registered trademarks of Scholastic Inc.

12 11 10 9 8 7 6 5 4 3 2   8 9/9 0 1 2 3/0

Printed in the U.S.A.   23

First Scholastic printing, February 1998

Hand lettering and design by Meredith Baldwin.

Contents

Hot Fudge Hero

Bertie and Mr. Muckleberg

The Bet

Mr. Muckleberg was
a mean old man.
He had a mean dog named Attila.
He had a mean cat named Screamer.
And he lived in a
mean-looking house with a
mean-looking wall
all around it.
Bertie lived next door.
One day Bertie
and his friend Isobel
were playing catch.

Bertie's ball went over the backyard wall.

It landed in Mr. Muckleberg's yard.

"You can say good-bye
to that ball," said Isobel.

"You will never get it back from
Old Man Muckleberg."

Bertie was not so sure.

He put a ladder on the wall.

He climbed up and looked down
into Mr. Muckleberg's yard.

There was tall grass
and a lot of weeds.
He saw an old red car
with one door hanging off.
He saw a broken hoe.
He saw an old boot
with a bird's nest in it.
He did not see his ball.
"You will never get it back,"
Isobel dared.
"Yes, I will," said Bertie.
"I bet you a hot fudge sundae
you won't," said Isobel.
"It's a deal," said Bertie.
"Today is Monday. You must
have the ball by Friday,"
said Isobel.
"Okay, by Friday," Bertie agreed.

Step One

That afternoon
Bertie and his mom
went to the library.
Bertie found a book.
It was called
How to Make Friends
in Five Easy Steps.
Bertie said,
"I will read this book.
I will make Mr. Muckleberg
my friend.
I will ask him to give me back

my ball.

I will win my bet with Isobel.

It will be easy."

He started to read the book.

Step One seemed simple.

"Be friendly. Say hello."

Bertie wanted to try it

as soon as he got home.

He walked up and down in front of

Mr. Muckleberg's house.

Attila growled at him.

Screamer hissed at him.

But he did not see Mr. Muckleberg.

"I will call him on the phone,"
Bertie said.

It rang five times.

"Hello," said Mr. Muckleberg
in a mean voice.

"Hi, Mr. Muckleberg!
This is Bertie, from next door."

"What do you want?"
Mr. Muckleberg asked.

"I just wanted to say hello,
Mr. Muckleberg.
Hello, and how are you today?"

"I am busy is how I am,"
said Mr. Muckleberg.
And he hung up the phone.

Bertie took a deep breath.
Then he smiled and said,
"That takes care of Step One."

Step Two

On Tuesday
Bertie looked at his book.
Step Two was
"Say something nice to your friend.
Make sure you mean it."
Bertie thought for a minute.
"This time I won't
use the phone," he said.
He took a piece of paper.
He made it into an airplane.
On the wings he wrote:

Dear Mr. Muckleberg,
You sure have a lot of interesting
things in your yard.

Your friend,
Bertie
(from next door)

He went upstairs to his room.

He opened the window and waited.

When Mr. Muckleberg came out

to feed Attila, Bertie took aim.

The plane went flying.

It flew right into

Attila's water dish.

Mr. Muckleberg picked up the plane.

He looked at the writing.

He looked at Bertie's house.

10

Bertie waved.

Mr. Muckleberg frowned.

Bertie smiled.

"I think Mr. Muckleberg
was going to smile,
but the sun got in his eyes
and made him frown."

"And that takes care of Step Two,"
Bertie said.

Just then the phone rang.

It was Isobel.

"Did you get your ball back yet?"
she asked.

"Not yet," said Bertie.

"But I'm working on it."

"You will never get it back
from Old Man Muckleberg,"
Isobel said.

"I will really enjoy the
hot fudge sundae you will buy me."

"Ha!" said Bertie.

"Just you wait.

I will get my ball back yet."

Step Three

On Wednesday Bertie read Step Three.

"Ask your new friend some questions.
Find out what he thinks
about things."

"Easy," said Bertie.

He got a can of tuna and opened it.

He filled a bowl with milk.

Then he went outside.

He climbed the ladder by the wall.

He put the tuna and milk
on top of the wall.

Mr. Muckleberg was in his yard.

"Hi, Mr. Muckleberg!

It's me, Bertie!"

Mr. Muckleberg frowned.

"Humpf!" he said.

"Nice day, isn't it?"

Bertie asked.

"Humpf!" said Mr. Muckleberg.

"Do you think it will rain?"

asked Bertie.

"Humpf!" said Mr. Muckleberg.

Then Bertie saw Screamer

coming along the top of the wall.

Screamer looked mean and hungry.

"Here, kitty," said Bertie.

"Here is some nice tuna and milk."

Screamer ate all the tuna

and drank all the milk.

"I think your cat likes me,

Mr. Muckleberg.

What do you think?"

"Humpf!" said Mr. Muckleberg.

"I guess that means

he thinks so, too,"

Bertie said to the cat.

Screamer just purred and purred.

Step Four

On Thursday
Bertie read Step Four.
*"Be polite and kind
to your new friend.
Ask him if there is some way
you can help him."*
Bertie got some meat loaf
and chicken from the kitchen.
He took it to Mr. Muckleberg's
front gate.
Attila jumped up.
He barked and snarled.

Bertie slid the meat loaf
under the gate.
Attila ate it in three gulps.
Bertie opened the gate.
He walked up to the front door.
Screamer leaped onto the porch
and hissed.
Bertie put the chicken on the floor.
By the time Mr. Muckleberg
opened the door,
Attila's bark was friendly
and Screamer was purring.
"Good morning, Mr. Muckleberg,"
Bertie said.
"Would you like me to take Attila
for a walk?"
Mr. Muckleberg stared at Bertie.

At last he said,

"Who is Attila?"

Bertie pointed to the animal

next to him.

"Attila," he said again,

"your dog."

Mr. Muckleberg almost smiled.

"Her name is not Attila,"

Mr. Muckleberg said.

Her name is Hilda.

I named her after

my second-grade teacher."

"I'm going into second grade,"

Bertie said.

"Is that so," said Mr. Muckleberg.

He began to close the door.

"Who did you name

Screamer after?" Bertie asked.

Mr. Muckleberg laughed

a small dry laugh.

"Do you know what they call

a cat who likes to catch mice?"

he asked.

Bertie shook his head.

"A mouser,"

Mr. Muckleberg told him.

"But this old cat
just likes to drink cream.
So I named her Creamer.
Not Screamer."
He laughed again
and shut the door.
Bertie scratched Hilda
behind the ears.
"We'll go for a walk
another day," he said.
Hilda thumped her tail
on the porch floor.

Step Five

On Friday, Isobel called Bertie.

"Do you have your ball back?"
Isobel asked.

"Not yet," Bertie said.

"But I'll get it soon."

"Today is Friday,"
Isobel said.

"And we had a deal.

Now you must buy me

a hot fudge sundae."

"Isobel, it's only noon.

Friday isn't over yet.

I said I would have it on Friday
and I will."
"So, what time will we go
for sundaes?" asked Isobel.
"Two o'clock," said Bertie.
"Come for me at two.
If I don't have my ball back,
I'll buy you a hot fudge sundae."
"With nuts," said Isobel.
"With nuts," Bertie said.
Time was running out.
If he was going to make
Mr. Muckleberg
his lifelong friend,
he had better hurry.
Bertie looked at Step Five.
*"Invite your friend to do something
with you. Have fun!"*

Bertie ate lunch.

He tried to think of something

he could do with Mr. Muckleberg.

Bertie didn't have his ball.

So they couldn't play catch.

He didn't think Mr. Muckleberg

owned a bike.

So they couldn't ride bikes.

At last Bertie knew what to do—
checkers!
He tucked the box of checkers
under his arm.
He went next door
and rang Mr. Muckleberg's doorbell.
"Hi, Mr. Muckleberg!
Would you like to play checkers?"
"Checkers, is it?" he asked.
He came out and sat
in an old rocker.
Bertie put the checkers
on the table next to it.
They played for a long time.
But Bertie still did not have
his ball.

Hot Fudge Sundaes

It was almost two o'clock.

Isobel would be coming over soon.

Bertie had done everything that

How to Make Friends

in Five Easy Steps said to do.

He was sure that Mr. Muckleberg

was now his lifelong friend.

It was time to ask for his ball.

"Mr. Muckleberg,

did you find a baseball

in your yard this week?"

Mr. Muckleberg only looked
at the checkerboard.
"No," he said.
"I didn't find a baseball."
"Oh," said Bertie.

It was over.
He had lost the bet.
Now he would have to buy
that hot fudge sundae for Isobel.

"I didn't find a baseball,"

Mr. Muckleberg said again.

"But Hilda did."

He pulled the ball from his pocket.

"Is this what you're

looking for?"

Bertie smiled.

"Thanks, Mr. Muckleberg.

Thanks a lot."

Just then Isobel came by.

Bertie held up the ball

for her to see.

"Darn!" said Isobel.

"Isobel and I had a bet,"

Bertie told Mr. Muckleberg.

"She bet I would not find my ball

by today.

Now she has to buy me
a hot fudge sundae."
Mr. Muckleberg looked at Isobel.
"You didn't think Old Man Muckleberg
would give it back, did you?"
Isobel's mouth fell open.
But Mr. Muckleberg laughed.
"Hot fudge sundaes, is it?
Why, I haven't had
a hot fudge sundae in years."
"Would you like to
come with us?" Bertie asked.
"Yes, I would," said Mr. Muckleberg.
"But only if I can treat."
"It's a deal!"
Bertie and Isobel said together.

Bertie smiled and thought,
The only thing better than
two lifelong friends
is
two lifelong friends
and ice cream.

Sax Magic

Bertie's Wish

SQUEAK! SCREECH! BLAT!

"It's no use!" Bertie said.

"I just can't do it!"

"Keep trying," said his dad.

"The saxophone isn't easy to play.

But you'll get better

if you practice."

SQUEAK! BLAT!

SCREECH! BLAT!

"Mom! Make him stop!

He's hurting my ears!"

yelled Bertie's younger sister, Eloise.

"I give up!" said Bertie.
He put the saxophone
down on the floor.
His mother called to him
from the kitchen.
"Are you done already?" she asked.
"I'm done forever," Bertie said.
"I'll never learn to play
the saxophone."

"Never is a long time,"
said his mother.
"You will learn if you
keep on trying."
But Bertie didn't want to
keep on trying.
He wanted to be able to play it
right away.
He went to his room
and lay down on his bed.
"If only I had a fairy godmother.
She could wave her magic wand
and make me able to play."

He closed his eyes
and went to sleep.
Bertie dreamed he was
in his living room.
He was practicing his saxophone.
The doorbell rang.
Bertie answered it.
A tall man was standing there.
He was dressed in black

and wore a hat pushed to the back
of his head.

"Hello," said Bertie.

"Who are you?"

"I'm your fairy godmother,"
the man said.

"You're a man," Bertie said.

"Men can't be fairy godmothers."

"Okay, then I'm your
fairy godfather," said the man.

"You don't look like
a fairy godfather," said Bertie.

"Where is your wand?
Where is your magic fairy dust?"

"Fairy dust, shmairy dust,"
said the man.

"You can't believe everything
you see in the movies.

Not all fairy godfathers
use wands and fairy dust."
"But what about your size?
I thought fairy godmothers
were small and floated on air."
"Fairy godmothers might be small
and float on air," said the man,
"but fairy godfathers are big
and stand on the ground."
"Sounds fishy to me," said Bertie.
"Well," said the man,
"if it seems so fishy,
tell me this—
did you or did you not
wish for a fairy godmother
to help you play the saxophone?"
"Wow!" said Bertie.
"I did wish for that.

I guess you are real,

after all."

"So, enough already

with all these questions,"

said the man.

"Let's get down to work.

May I come in?" he asked.

"Of course," said Bertie.

The Fairy Godfather's Advice

They went into the living room.

The man sat down on the couch.

"Let me hear you play," he said.

"If I could play," said Bertie,

"I wouldn't have wished for

a fairy godmother."

"Okay," said the man,

"then let me hear you try to play."

"Hold your ears," said Bertie.

He picked up the saxophone.

He put the mouthpiece in his mouth

and blew.

SQUEAK!
BLAT!
SCREECH!
"Okay, I've heard enough,"
said the man.
"Now listen to my advice."
He talked to Bertie about
the way to hold his fingers.

He told him how to hold his mouth
and blow.
He told him how to take care of
his reed and saxophone.
"This is good advice," said Bertie.
"But what about the magic?"
The man took off his hat and put it
on Bertie's head.
"The magic is in the hat," he said.
"You must do all the things
I have told you about.
And if you wear the hat,
you'll play like a pro."
"Okay," said Bertie. "I'll try."
"That is what I want," said the man.
"I just want you to keep on trying."
He got up and headed for the door.

"Before you go," Bertie said,

"may I ask you one more thing?"

"Sure," said the man.

"What do you want to know?"

"Your name," Bertie said.

"Stan," the man told him.

"You can call me Stan."

Bertie smiled.

"Thanks, Stan.

Thanks a lot."

"Sure, kid," Stan said.

"Anytime.

And remember—

there is fast magic in the hat,

but there is slow magic in you."

Before Bertie could ask

what that meant,

Stan was gone.

When Bertie woke up

he felt something lumpy

under his head.

He sat up and looked at his pillow.

"The hat!" said Bertie.

He thought about his dream.

He remembered all the things

Stan had told him.

He put on the hat and

went to get his saxophone.

Bertie Gets Better

Every day Bertie played
his saxophone.
When he wore the hat,
he sounded terrific.
Even his sister, Eloise, liked it.
When he did not wear the hat,
there were squeaks.
There were screeches.
There were blats.
Then Eloise would hold her ears
and complain.
Every day Bertie played

"Old MacDonald."

With the hat on,

he was terrific!

He played again with the hat off.

He was not so terrific.

He played

"I've Been Working on the Railroad."

With the hat,

he was terrific.

Without the hat,

he was not so terrific.

Day after day

Bertie played.

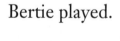

And then one day
he noticed something.
With the hat on,
he was still terrific.
But now,
without the hat,
he was not quite so bad.
He was still not terrific,
but he was getting better.

Passing on the Magic

One day Bertie

was walking home from school.

The sun was shining.

The birds were singing.

He opened the front door.

He heard **SCREECH!**

BLAT! SQUEAK!

"I know what that means," Bertie said.

He went upstairs to his room.

"Hey!" he said to Eloise.

"Who said you could play

my saxophone?"

"Come on, Bertie,

please let me.

I want to play like you."

"I thought you said

it hurt your ears,"

Bertie told her.

"When you play,

it doesn't hurt my ears.

But when I play—
yikes!
Help me, Bertie. Please?"
Bertie looked at Eloise.
At last he smiled.
"Okay," he said.
"Listen to me.
Here is what you must do."
Bertie told Eloise
how to hold her fingers.
He told her how to
hold her mouth and blow.
He told her how to take care of
the reed and the saxophone.
"And," he said,
"you must ask Mom and Dad
if you can take lessons."

"All these things
are good to know,"
said Eloise.
"But I still won't
be able to play.
Listen."
She started to play.

DAH, DAH, SQUEAK, DAH,
SCREECH, SQUEAK, BLAT!

"Hmm," said Bertie.

"There is one more thing."

He reached up and

took off his hat.

He held the hat

and looked at it.

He thought,

When I wear the hat,

I am terrific.

When I do not wear the hat,

I am not so terrific,

but I am getting better.

Then he understood what Stan meant

about fast magic and slow magic.

"Here," said Bertie.

He put the hat on Eloise's head.

"There is fast magic in the hat.

When you wear it,

you will play like a pro.

But there is slow magic

in you."

"What do you mean?" asked Eloise.

Bertie only smiled.

"You'll find out," he said.

Eloise played

"Twinkle, Twinkle, Little Star."

She was terrific!

"Wow!" said Eloise.

"It really *is* magic!

Thanks, Bertie.

Thanks a lot."

Bertie smiled.

"Sure, kid," he said.

"Anytime."

Bertie started to

leave the room.

"Wait!" Eloise called.

She took off the hat

and looked at it

for a long time.

"What's the matter?"

Bertie asked.

"Just this," said Eloise.

"You have given me something

very special.

I would like to give you

something special, too."

Bertie smiled.

"Okay," he said.

"What would you like to give me?"

he asked.

Eloise smiled back.

"It's not as special as

a magic hat,"

she told him.

"But it's the next best thing."

"Hot fudge sundaes!"

they both said together.

Turkey Day

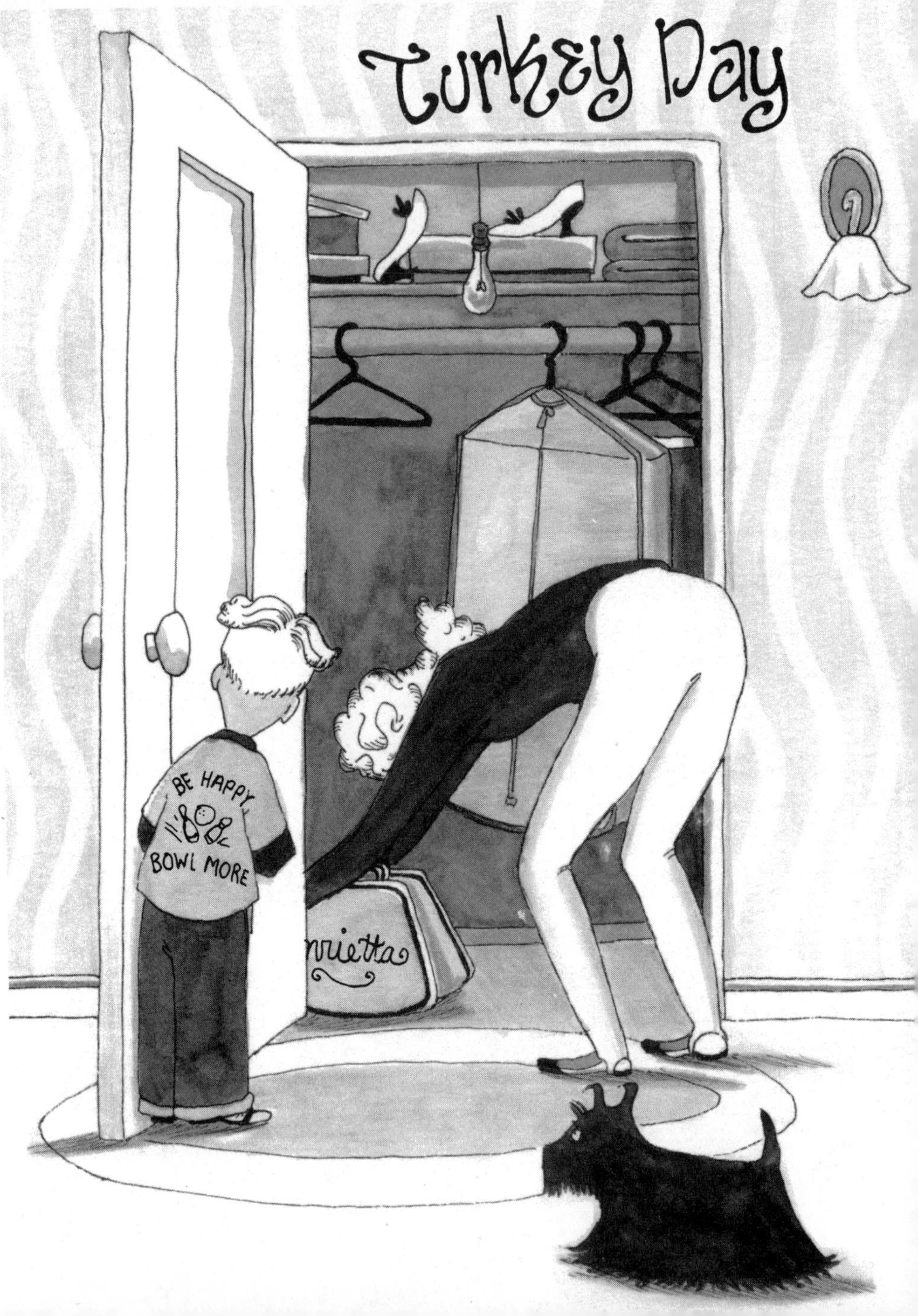

Getting Ready

On Saturday
Bertie's mom woke him up.
"Bowling day!" she said.
Bertie got out of bed right away.
"Maybe today I'll get a strike!"
he said to his mother.
A strike is when you knock over
ten pins with the first ball.
"A strike would be nice," Mom said,
"but a spare is nice, too."
A spare is when you knock over
some of the pins with the first ball
and the rest with the second ball.

"I've had spares," Bertie told her,

"but I've never had a strike."

"Today feels like a lucky day," Mom said.

"Today you just might get

that strike.

And maybe I will get a turkey."

A turkey is three strikes in a row.

"Gobble, gobble!" Mom said.

She flapped her arms like a turkey.

"Gobble, gobble, gobble!"

Bertie answered.

He got dressed quickly.

He put on his bowling shirt.

It has BERTIE in red letters

over the pocket.

On the back are bowling pins

being hit by a bowling ball

and the words: BE HAPPY! BOWL MORE!

Mom got Henrietta
from the hall closet.
Henrietta is Mom's bowling ball.
She is shiny dark purple
and her name is painted on
with white fancy letters.
For a bowling ball,
Henrietta is very beautiful.
Before they left,
they said good-bye to Waldo.
"Good-bye, Waldo! Wish us luck!"
Waldo barked and
thumped his tail on the floor.
That meant, "Get a strike!"
Waldo is one smart dog.

At the Alley

The bowling alley was noisy.

Balls rolled. Pins got knocked down.

People talked and laughed.

Bertie and his mother rented bowling shoes.

They were given lane seven.

But first Bertie had to find Thunderhawk.

Thunderhawk is the name Bertie gave

to the bowling ball he uses.

It belongs to the bowling alley

but it's always on a rack

waiting for him to find it.

Thunderhawk is forest green

with silver streaks.

No other balls are like Thunderhawk.

Bertie hunted and hunted.

He couldn't find Thunderhawk anywhere.

Finally, he had to choose

another ball.

That took a long time.

He picked up a lot of balls

that were too heavy.

At last he found one.

It wasn't shiny purple

like Henrietta.

It wasn't forest green

with silver streaks

like Thunderhawk.

It was orange,

plain old, ugly orange.

"I hate orange," Bertie said.

"Now I'll never get a strike."

"Maybe you won't,

but maybe you will," Mom said.

"You'll never know unless you try."

Bertie started to complain again,

but Mom snapped, "Bertie!"

And he knew what that voice meant:

It was time to bowl.

The First Game

Mom bowled first.

She held the ball in front of her.

She took three steps,

swung her arm backward and forward,

and sent the ball down the alley.

Crack!

It hit the pins. Seven went down.

She waited for the ball

to come back to her.

Then she rolled it again.

Crack!

She got two more down.

Then it was Bertie's turn.

He picked up the ugly orange ball.

It was heavier than Thunderhawk.

He swung it back and forth

to get used to the way it felt.

He rolled it down the alley.

It fell from his hand with a loud thud.

About halfway down the alley

it rolled to the side

and landed in the gutter.

Gutter balls don't get any points.

"I hate this ball!" Bertie said.

"It's ugly and it's too heavy."

"You're not used to it yet,"
Mom said. "Try again."
The ugly orange ball
had come back to him.
He picked it up and rolled it again.
Another gutter ball.
"Take your time, Bertie.
You're not even trying."
"Yes, I am," Bertie told her.
"It's the dumb ball's fault."
Mom went again and got a strike.
"All that gobbling
must have helped," she said.
"It hasn't helped me," Bertie said.
"Then we better keep at it," Mom shouted.
And then she started gobbling
and flapping her arms
right there at the bowling alley.

"Mom!

Everybody's looking at you!" Bertie said.

"Then bowl better, Bertie,

because I'm going to keep up

this good-luck gobbling until you do!"

She laughed and kept gobbling.

Bertie knew she wouldn't stop

until he started bowling better.

He picked up the ugly orange ball.

He kept his eyes on the pins
and rolled the ball.
It started to go to the gutter
but then came back.
It didn't roll as fast as Mom's,
but at least it got
to the end of the alley.
Thump! It hit one pin
and then another
and those pins knocked down
two more pins.
"See?" said Mom.
"This good-luck gobbling works!"

The Second Game

The ugly ball didn't seem

as heavy by the second game.

Bertie was getting fewer gutter balls.

So Mom was doing less gobbling.

A few times Bertie almost

got a strike,

but then the ball moved a little bit

and only knocked down some of the pins.

By the middle of the game

Mom had gotten two strikes in a row.

One more strike and

she would have her turkey.

When her turn came,
she started gobbling again.
She walked like a turkey
to her bowling ball.
She looked back at Bertie.
"Let's hear some gobbling
over there," Mom said.
So Bertie started gobbling, too.
Mom laughed and rolled the ball.
It rolled fast, right toward the first pin.
Crack! A strike!
Three in a row!
Mom had gotten her turkey!
But would Bertie get his strike?
He rolled the ball
and hit seven pins.
His next ball went straight
into the gutter.

"Maybe today is just not
my day," Bertie sighed.
"The day isn't over yet," Mom told him.
When it was Bertie's turn again,
he didn't get a strike.
But he did get eight pins down.
And on the next roll,
he got the last two down,
so he got a spare.
Mom got up again.
She got eight pins down.
Bertie went to get his ball.
It didn't look as ugly now.
It wasn't as nice as Thunderhawk,
but he had bowled
pretty well with it after all.
He picked it up
and thought about Mom's turkey.

"If Mom can do it,

so can I," Bertie said.

"Gobble, gobble," Mom called.

"Get a strike," Bertie told himself.

He rolled the ball.

It didn't wobble. It didn't curve.

It headed right for the pins.

He held his breath.

Crack!

Nine pins fell down right away.

The last one wobbled back and forth.

Bertie knew what he had to do.

"Gobble! Gobble!" he said.

"Gobble! Gobble! Gobble! Gobble . . ."

At last, it fell over.

A strike!

Bertie had gotten a strike!

"Hooray!" his mom yelled.

"You did it, Bertie!"

"We both did it!" Bertie said.

Packing Up

Mom and Bertie got ready to leave.

Bertie took the ugly orange ball

back to its rack.

It needed a name, too.

He thought for a minute.

"Lucky," he said at last.

"I'm going to call you Lucky."

And he decided that next week

he would look for Lucky again

and leave Thunderhawk for someone else.

They paid for their games

and went out to the parking lot.

"Your first strike!" Mom said.

She smiled at Bertie

and put her arm around him.

"Your first turkey!" Bertie said,

and smiled back at her.

"Let's go out to celebrate!" Mom said.

"Hot fudge sundaes?" Bertie asked.

"Okay," Mom said.

"But first, sandwiches for lunch."

"Good idea," said Bertie.

"And I know exactly

what kind of sandwiches

we should get."

"So do I," Mom said.

"TURKEY!" they shouted together.

And they gobble, gobble, gobbled

all the way there.

The End